The Magic Beans

DEAR CAREGIVER,

The *Beginning-to-Read* series is a carefully written collection of classic readers you may remember from your own childhood. Each book features text comprised of common sight words to provide your child ample practice reading the words that appear most frequently in written text. The many additional details in the pictures enhance the story and offer the opportunity for you to help your child expand oral language and develop comprehension.

Begin by reading the story to your child, followed by letting him or her read familiar words and soon your child will be able to read the story independently. At each step of the way, be sure to praise your reader's efforts to build his or her confidence as an independent reader. Discuss the pictures and encourage your child to make connections between the story and his or her own life. At the end of the story, you will find reading activities and a word list that will help your child practice and strengthen beginning reading skills.

Above all, the most important part of the reading experience is to have fun and enjoy it!

Shannon Cannon

Shannon Cannon,
Literacy Consultant

Norwood House Press • P.O. Box 316598 • Chicago, Illinois 60631
For more information about Norwood House Press please visit our website at
www.norwoodhousepress.com or call 866-565-2900.

LIBRARY OF CONGRESS CATALOGING-IN-PUBLICATION DATA
  Hillert, Margaret.
    The magic beans / by Margaret Hillert ; illustrated by Mel Pekarsky.—
  Rev. and expanded library ed.
      p. cm. — (Beginning to read series. Fairy tales and folklore)
    Summary: Reading activities accompany this retelling of "Jack and the Beanstalk."
    ISBN-13: 978-1-59953-025-3 (library edition : alk. paper)
    ISBN-10: 1-59953-025-2 (library edition : alk. paper)
    [1. Fairy tales. 2. Folklore--England. 3. Giants--Folklore. 4. Readers.]
  I. Pekarsky, Mel, 1934- ill. II. Title. III. Series.
    PZ8.H5425Mac 2006
    [398.2]—dc22   2005033497

A Beginning-to-Read Book

The Magic Beans

by Margaret Hillert

Illustrated by Mel Pekarsky

NORWOOD HOUSE PRESS

5

Oh, look.
Here is something funny.
One is red.
One is blue.
One is yellow.

One little one.
Two little ones.
Three little ones.
Look, look, look.

Go down here.
Go down in here, little ones.

Oh, oh.
Look and see.
Here is something little.
Up it comes.

Oh, my. Oh, my.
It is big, big, big.

I can go up.
See me go up.
Up, up, up and away.

Look here, look here.
I see a house.
It is a big, big house.

I want to go in.
In I go.
Jump, jump, jump.

It is big in here.
It is big for little me.

Here is something.
It is not big.
It is little and red.

Look, look.
It can work.
It can make something.

Come to me.
Come to me.
I want you.
Come to my house.
Away we go.

Oh, look here.
Here is something for Mother.
Something for my mother.

And here is something.
We can play it.
We can make it play.
It is fun to play.

Come, come.
Come to my house.
Come to my mother.

Here we go.
Away, away, away.

Oh, my.
Here comes something.
Something big.
Where can I go?

Help, help.
Here I go.
Run, run, run.

And here I go.
Down, down, down.
Mother, Mother.
Here I come.
Help me. Help me.

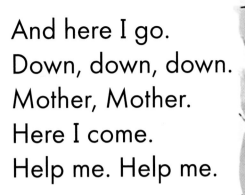

We can work.
We can make it come down.

Here, Mother.
Here is something for you.

The following activities support the findings of the National Reading Panel that determined the most effective components for reading instruction are: Phonemic Awareness, Phonics, Vocabulary, Fluency, and Text Comprehension.

Phonemic Awareness: The /b/ sound

Oddity Task: Say the /**b**/ sound for your child (be careful not to say buh). Say the following words aloud. Ask your child to say the words that do not end with the /**b**/ sound in the following word groups:

| tab, tap, tub | ball, bat, cab | cub, job, bus | bean, crib, bib |
| sob, cub, big | crab, bad, grab | bump, sob, knob | scrub, bun, club |

Phonics: The letter Bb

1. Demonstrate how to form the letters **B** and **b** for your child.
2. Have your child practice writing **B** and **b** at least three times each.
3. Ask your child to point to the words in the book that begin with the letter **b**.
4. Write down the following words and ask your child to circle the letter **b** in each word:

| barn | boot | lab | cab | bubble | bed | bib |
| bag | nibble | bone | crumble | bean | dab | thimble |

Vocabulary: Opposites

1. The story features the concepts of big and little. Discuss opposites and ask your child name the opposites of the following:

hot (cold)　　near (far)　　short (tall)
soft (hard)　　front (back)　　happy (sad)